THE SANNYASI & THE VEDAS

Saurabh Suman

Ukiyoto Publishing

All global publishing rights are held by

Ukiyoto Publishing

Published in 2024

Content Copyright © Saurabh Suman

ISBN 9789364941433

All rights reserved.
No part of this publication may be reproduced, transmitted, or stored in a retrieval system, in any form by any means, electronic, mechanical, photocopying, recording or otherwise, without the prior permission of the publisher.

The moral rights of the author have been asserted.

This book is sold subject to the condition that it shall not by way of trade or otherwise, be lent, resold, hired out or otherwise circulated, without the publisher's prior consent, in any form of binding or cover other than that in which it is published.

www.ukiyoto.com

To Mother, Motherland & Mother Tongue

Contents

CHAPTER ONE - Swami Vivekanand	1
CHAPTER TWO - Swami Vivekananda	3
CHAPTER THREE - Best Conversation	5
CHAPTER FOUR - The Calculation	13
CHAPTER FIVE - Swami Savior of Hinduism	23
CHAPTER SIX - The Smritis and The Puranas	26
CHAPTER SEVEN - Vedas-Introduction	28
CHAPTER EIGHT - Vedas	30
CHAPTER NINE - Sprituality Philosophy	35
About the Author	*39*

CHAPTER ONE
Swami Vivekanand

Hindu monk Swami Vivekananda was one of India's most renowned spiritual figures. He was more than just a spiritual thinker; he was also a prolific writer, an outstanding public speaker, and a fervent patriot.

At the time Swami Vivekananda visited England, there was a lot of racism there. Before World War 2, this occurred.

He was detested by a white professor with the surname name of Peters.

Mr. Peters once arrived with his tray and sat down next to the professor while the professor was having lunch in the dining room. Mr. Vivekanand, you don't understand, the professor said.

Pigs and birds do not eat in the same dining room. You should not be concerned, professor, Vivekanand gently replied like a father would a child who was being disrespectful. I'll fly away," he said as he walked over to a different table.

Red-faced with wrath, Mr. Peters made the decision to exact revenge. The following day in class, he said, "Mr. Vivekanand, which would you select if you were strolling down the street and you found some money on one side and a book of wisdom on the other side, and you had the choice?

Vivekanand answered without hesitation, "I will pick up the money, of course."

In response, Mr. Peters sarcastically grinned and stated, "I, in your place, would have taken the wisdom."

In response, Swami Vivekanand shrugged and said, "Sir, a person will pick up what he doesn't have."

By this point, Mr. Peters was ready to be bound. His rage was so intense that he scrawled the word "idiot" on Swami Vivekanand's exam sheet and delivered it to the spiritual leader. As he sat down at his desk, Vivekanand took the exam sheet.

A short while afterward, Swami Vivekanand stood up, approached the professor, and said, "Mr. Peters, you signed the sheet, but you did not give me the grade." in a respectful and courteous manner.

CHAPTER TWO
Swami Vivekananda

Swami Vivekananda's brilliant mind delved deeply into almost every area of human greatness and produced startling insights. His understanding of the subtleties of probability theory in statistics is less well-known, though. This article provides us with a glimpse into this previously unexplored facet of Swamiji.

It's possible that English terms for greatness are competing to capture Swami Vivekananda's multifaceted personality. Whatever the case, Swami Vivekananda transcends categorization. His place in global religious history would have been sealed had he simply given that incomparably felicitous address in Chicago on September 11, 1893. If his unique presentation of the four yogas—Jnana, Bhakti, Raja, and Karma—and their integration had been his sole contribution to the development of world thinking, he would have been hailed as the forerunner of synthesis. He would have been remembered as the innovator of a fresh take on monasticism even if he had merely founded the Ramakrishna Math and the Ramakrishna Mission. He would be recognized today as the creator of a new genre in Bengali literature even if his only contribution to the world of literature had been his well-known travelogue written in everyday Bengali. We are really fortunate that he provided us with everything mentioned above, as well as so much more. This is proof of the incredible soul force's ability to work across a range of human endeavors. It makes sense that this "prophet of infinity" plays a mind-boggling variety of roles, including those of a religious teacher, philosopher, historian, nationalist, social and economic thinker, litterateur, humorist, musician, sportsman, and more.

CHAPTER THREE
Best Conversation

What were the most memorable exchanges or tales between Ramkrishna Paramhansa and Swami Vivekanand?

More intense than any other human interaction, the bond between a guru and pupil is one of profound love.

We know that Shri Ramakrishna frequently

experienced divine visions and that Naren was a member of the Brahmo Samaj. How did their initial interaction go?

As evidence of the Master's lack of self-control, he (Swami Vivekananda) enjoyed critiquing his spiritual experiences. He mocked his devotion to Kali.

"What brings you here? 'If you do not accept Kali, my mother?' Sri Ramakrishna once questioned him.

'Bah! Naren responded, "Do I have to accept her just because I came to meet you? Because I adore you, I came to you.

Okay, the Master responded. Soon you will grieve in the name of my Blessed Mother in addition to accepting Her.

He then addressed his fellow followers, saying, "This boy has no confidence in the forms of God and claims that my visions are just a product of my imagination. But he is a fine young man with a good mind. Without concrete evidence, he will not accept anything. He has done a lot of reading and training in discrimination. He makes wise decisions.

Naren is known to have repeatedly tested his Guru. Has the Guru tested Naren as well?

On the other hand, the master frequently put Naren to the test. One day, he entered the master bedroom and received zero attention. There was no greeting spoken. He returned a week later and encountered the same lack of interest, and on his third and fourth visits, he observed no signs of the master's icy disposition warming up.

Naren, as we all know, frequently betrayed his Guru. The Guru also put Naren to the test.

The master, on the other hand, frequently put Naren to the test. One day, he went into the master bedroom and got no response. Not a single word of greeting was spoken. He returned a week later and was greeted with the same coldness, and on his third and fourth visits, he observed no signs of the master's attitude melting.

After a month had passed, Sri Ramakrishna addressed Naren, saying, "I haven't spoken to you in all this time, yet you come."

"I come to Dakshineswar because I love you and want to see you," the disciple retorted. I didn't come here to hear what you had to say.

The Master was ecstatic. I was just testing you, he remarked as he hugged the disciple. I wanted to see if my apparent disinterest would cause you to stay away. Only a man with your inner fortitude could tolerate my lack of interest. Any other person would have abandoned me long ago.

Did the Guru provide his attractive disciple any bait?

Sri Ramakrishna once advocated giving Narendranath many of the spiritual abilities he had attained as a result of his ascetic practices and God-seeking visions.

Naren was certain that the master possessed these abilities. If they could aid him in realizing God, he enquired. In response, Sri Ramakrishna said no, but added that they might help him in his upcoming career as a spiritual teacher.

Naren said, "Let me first discover God, and then I might know whether or not I want superhuman abilities. If I accept them now, I might forget God, use them selfishly, and suffer as a result.

The steadfast devotion of his primary student filled Sri Ramakrishna with great joy.

Did the Guru reprimand the famous disciple at all, and how did the Guru respond?

When Naren made a similar plea to stay in Samadhi on another occasion, Sri Ramakrishna responded, "Shame on you! You are requesting such a trivial thing. I imagined that thousands of people would seek refuge in your shade and that you would resemble a large banyan tree. However, I can now see that you are aiming for your own liberation.

As he was reprimanded, Narendra sobbed bitterly. He came to understand Sri Ramakrishna's nobility of heart.

When the disciple became the Great Master, did He extend this instruction to His disciples?

You will go to hell if you pursue your own salvation, the Swami warned a disciple who desired to practice spiritual discipline in order to secure his own salvation. If you desire to get to the highest level, work for the salvation of others. Put an end to the quest for individual mukti.

The best spiritual practice is this. Children, work with all your heart and soul! The issue is that. Don't worry about the results of your labor. What if working for others causes you to go to hell? That is more valuable than obtaining heaven through personal salvation. Sri Ramakrishna arrived and sacrificed his life for all people. I'll also give my life in sacrifice. Every single one of you should follow suit.

These projects and others are just the beginning. You better believe that from the blood we spilt will come mighty, heroic laborers and God's fighters who will alter the entire planet.

Swami Vivekananda

Ah, and the aforementioned phrases served as the cornerstone of what is now known as Shri

Ramakrishna Mission, the world's silent, non-trumpeting powerhouse and beacon. The same idea is shared by every monk I am aware of on the trip. All of you!

Naren's last remaining concern was if the master's fragile body would succumb at any moment. Naren, oh Naren!

Narendra was sitting at the Master's bedside two days before the body of the latter began to dissolve when he had an odd thought: Was the Master really an Incarnation of God?

If the Master declared himself to be an incarnation as he stood on the verge of death, he said to himself, then I will acknowledge Sri Ramakrishna's divinity. However, this was just a fleeting thought.

He stood and fixed his eyes on the master's face. Eventually, Sri Ramakrishna separated his lips and exclaimed, "O my Naren, are you still not persuaded?" in a loud voice. Though not from the perspective of your Vedanta, "He who in the past was born as Rama and Krishna is now residing in this very body as Ramakrishna."

(Vedanta declares that everyone is God, and Shri Ramakrishna specifically stated that this is not just in accordance with this Vedanta.)

Any predictions made by the Guru regarding the pupil, then?

Narendra would give up his body of his own free will, the guru later told the other disciples. He will decline to remain on this planet once he understands his actual nature. He is about to unleash his intellectual and spiritual might on the world.

I have prayed to the Divine Mother to preserve him from knowing the absolute and to drape a veil of maya over his eyes. He still has a lot of work to do. However, the curtain appears to be so thin that it could break at any moment.

Shri Ramakrishna Paramahamsa

Has the prophecy been realized?

Yes, the first part became a resounding truth, which is known to everyone.

How about the second component?

Moving on, a few weeks before the Great Swami Vivekananda's sacrifice of his body,

He was fascinated with Sri Ramakrishna and the Divine Mother. He pretended to be a mother's child or a young boy playing at Sri Ramakrishna's feet at Dakshineswar.

"A great tapasya and meditation have come upon me, and I am preparing for death," he (Swami Vivekananda) declared.

His pensive attitude alarmed his followers and spiritual brothers. They recalled Sri Ramakrishna's assertion that Naren would cease to exist in his physical form if he discovered who he truly was and that, after his mission was fulfilled, he would merge permanently into samadhi.

One day, a fellow monk questioned him in a casual manner, "Do you know yet who you are?"

Everyone in attendance was astonished by the unexpected response, "Yes, I now know!"

No more inquiries were made.

Everyone recalled the epic Nirvikalpa samadhi of Naren's youth and how Sri Ramakrishna had declared at its conclusion, "Now the Mother has shown you everything."

But I'll keep this understanding to myself and keep it hidden from you, much like a treasure that's locked in a box. I'll always have the key on me. The box won't be opened until you've completed your task here on earth, at which point you'll be aware of all the information you currently know.

All of the aforementioned are taken from one single book, "Vivekananda: A Biography," written by Swami Nikhilananda.

For this reason, I kindly ask everyone to read Shri Ramakrishna and Swami Vivekananda's spiritual writings.

Strength, emotional balance, purpose, spirituality, and unending grace be with you, whoever reads them—this will be your life's greatest guiding light!

Where else can you discover these words of power and fervor that bless and encourage everyone to spirituality and a wise existence in the world?

Unless Shiva Himself says them, where else can they be found?

The Vedas proclaim, "The sannyasi stands on the head of the Vedas!" because he is exempt from denominations, sects, faiths, prophets, and texts.

He is God as we can see him. Keep this in mind as you boldly walk your journey as a sannyasin, bearing the banner of renunciation—the banner of peace, freedom, and blessing!

Love him and keep him close to your hearts! His heart is softer than the wind, his words are more powerful than fire, and his feet are unquestionably those of Shiva!

CHAPTER FOUR
The Calculation

While Albert Einstein, a famous theoretical physicist, refused to have God play dice with the cosmos out of respect for nature's inevitability, Swami Vivekananda, possibly the greatest advocate for God, believed that the creator was a consummate ice player! Intriguingly, Swamiji's attribution of dice-playing to God does not render Him (God) a capricious creature; rather, what emerges in and through God's created universe is a "specialized" deterministic pattern, driven by the "law of chance." The secular science of probability has undoubtedly never previously or subsequently been given such a revered status!The setting in which Swamiji addresses probability theory is as stimulating as it is possible to be. He was addressing an American audience when he discussed immortality. It's obvious that the subject had everyone listening intently to what he had to say. Who doesn't desire eternal life? It is pointless to dispute that the "literal" meaning of immortality is what fascinates people, even though different religious traditions may elaborate on its "implied" meaning (i.e., that the spiritual self is immortal). Nobody can help but ponder: Can I live eternally as the 'person' that I am now? Theological traditions can only at best predict an afterlife in paradise since they lack an explanation.

But Swamiji stepped up to the plate. He then went on to demonstrate how even constituted entities can repeat, although at specific periodic intervals, using an argument that is a logical masterwork in and of itself. He organized his facts like a skilled probabilist:

"Bodies and shapes are even immortal in a certain sense. How? Let's say we toss a bunch of dice and they land in the following order: 6—5—3—4. The same numbers must appear again at some point, as well as the same combination, so we continue to toss the dice. Now, I take each atom and particle in this cosmos as a die, and these are being discarded and merged once more.

There are several forms in front of you. The shapes of a glass, a table, a pitcher of water, and other objects are seen here. This particular combo will eventually disintegrate. However, the exact identical circumstances must arise again at some point when you, this form, this topic, and this pitcher are all present at the same moment. This has been done an infinite number of times, and it will be done an unlimited number of times more.

The careful reader will not miss the fact that the entire argument hinges on the extensive replications of the experiment involving throwing dice and the assurance of the recurrence of a set of outcomes that occurred at a specific throw. Now, a person with a decent amount of familiarity with probability theory can draw the conclusion that a certain set will undoubtedly repeat in a series of random occurrences (i.e., "there must be a time when the same numbers will come again"). With reference to Swamiji's example of simultaneously tossing four dice and noting an outcome of 6, 5, 3, 4, we might as well attempt to follow his train of thought here. If the experiment of throwing the four dice is performed a lot of times, the probabilist in Swamiji claims that this result must happen again ('We take the dice up and throw them again and again.'). What led him to this conclusion?

Here is the quick calculation, and a few prior assumtions that may have flashed through his extraordinary intellect:

While the great theoretical
Physicist Albert Einstein
fear of vitiating nature's
determinism—would not have
God is playing dice with the
universe, Swami Vivekananda
arguably the greatest champion
of God—found the creator to be
a consummate dice player!

The probability that the outcomes 6, 5, 3, and 4 do not occur in any of the 'n' experiments is $(1 - 1/64)$ n, or $(1295/1296)n$, assuming that (a) each die is fair, meaning that its six faces are equally likely to occur (b) the experiment of simultaneously casting four dice is repeated 'n' times (c) the outcomes of each of the four dice in any experiment are independent (d), and (e) all the 'n' experiments are independent. The probability that the collection of numbers 6, 5, 3, and 4 happens at least once is now $1 - (1295/1296)^n$. The likelihood that the set of 6, 5, 3, and 4 will occur at least once decreases as 'n' increases and trends towards 1, or certainty! In actuality, this chance is roughly 0.9995 for n = 10,000.

Voila! It is quite astonishing how Swamiji used this emerging science of chance—at least as it existed in the 19th century—to make some previously unheard-of observations on the immortality of bodies and forms, hastily pointing out that "that is not the immortality of the soul." Nevertheless, as the aim of this essay is to comprehend Swamiji as a probabilist, we will limit our discussion to the immortality of bodies and forms, on which Swamiji so deftly applies the "Law of Chance." Another lecture, titled "The Atman: Its Bondage and Freedom," features a similar illustration of the same concept with the addition of a probability theory concept: "All the forms we are seeing today have repeatedly manifested, and the world in which we live has existed previously. I've spoken to you several times previously while I've been here. Since you have already heard these words many times before, you will understand that it must be true. It will remain the same time after time. Souls have always been the same, and bodies have been continuously vanishing and reappearing. Second, these occurrences are regular. When we throw three or four dice, let's say one comes up five, another four, another three, and another two.

If you keep tossing, eventually the exact same numbers will come up again. Continue throwing, and those numbers will eventually return, regardless of how lengthy the pause was. This is a matter of chance; it is impossible to predict how often they will return. In light of spirits and their connections No matter how far apart the times are, identical combinations and dissolutions will continually take place.

In the aforementioned example, Swamiji not only asserts that the die combinations 5, 4, 3, and 2 will undoubtedly occur at some point in the future, but he also makes a comment about how many throws could be necessary to get the identical combination again. It would be wise to revisit the following observation: This is a matter of chance; it is impossible to predict how often they will return. We can speculate that the printed words in Vol. II of the Complete Works may be a little bit of an inadequate portrayal of what the probabilist-sannyasi intended to say. We'll make an educated guess after trying to reason it out using logic and evidence and leave it at that.

Amazing how Swamiji does things used this developing science of making some decisions in the past unusual comments on Body "immortality" and forms, quickly highlighting nonetheless, "that is not the case" eternal life for the soul.

One reason is that the phrases "This is the law of chance" and "It cannot be asserted in how many throws they will come again" are slightly contradictory. It is ipso facto true that the number of throws can be declared if a "law" is in effect. To state the opposite is to defy reason. Even if it is the "law of chance," rather than a deterministic law, an emphatic "cannot be asserted" contradicts the idea of "predictability" that is implied in the word "law."

More crucially, we have reason to assume that Swamiji's 'spoken' comments on this issue (likely recorded fairly verbatim by Mr. J.J. Goodwin) are quite different and are in fact more in line with the particular application of probability theory that he was endorsing. The following is an excerpt from Mr. Goodwin's transcript of the same lecture, "The Atman: Its Bondage and Freedom," which differs in some places from the corresponding paragraph in the Complete Works:

Let's say there are three or four dice, and when we throw them, one shows a five, then another four, then another three, then another two, and so on.

Eventually, the exact same numbers must appear again. Continue throwing, and those numbers will eventually return, regardless of how lengthy the pause was. The law of chance states that they will arrive again after a certain number of throws.

Since probability theory has not yet been

acknowledged as a separate field from mathematics, Swamiji must have been using these two terms almost interchangeably as a matter of loose convention. If we were to read "mathematically" as "probabilistically" in the italicized sentence above, it would be clear that Swamiji meant "the number of throws" necessary to have the repetition of the outcomes 5, 4, 3, 2.

Rather than stating the precise value of throws, Swamiji essentially conveyed the 'anticipated value' of them. While it is impossible to determine the precise number of throws in a random process (a process in which the law of chance is in play), it is possible to get an "average" number of throws using the rule of probability. In the language of probability, this is referred to as the "expected value." Let's try to understand what Swamiji was alluding to: Four dice are being thrown at once in this scenario. The results of the first throw are 5, 4, 3, and 2. Let's label this result as a "success" in the subsequent throws and any other result as a "failure."Let's further assume that p represents the success probability. Therefore, the likelihood of failure is (1-p). We are curious about the throw number at which the next success happens given this configuration. Now, if X is defined as the thrown number at which the next success occurs (rather, a random variable as the underlying experiment is random), the necessary probability that the next success occurs at X=x, assuming that the first success occurred at the first throw, is:

P (X=x|The first throw is a success) = $p(1-p)^{x-2}$; x=2,3,......∞

It's easy to verify that the above is a probability mass function as

Now, the throw number at which the second success happens would fairly be represented by this predicted value (1+1/p). If each die is assumed to be equally fair, then p = 1/64. In that example, (1 + 64) = 1297 is the average throw number at which the second success occurs. Our expert guess is that when Swamiji said, "It can be mathematically asserted in how many throws they will come again; this is the law of chance," he meant this predicted value of throws.

The discussion that just took place shows how Swamiji handled some of the key probability theory ideas with apparent ease.It is all the more remarkable that a sannyasi could grasp this pretty complex theory almost to the point of skill given that it was only known to the most elite intellectual circles of the nineteenth century. This level of skill led to an unreserved compliment from none other than Dr. John Venn of the University of Cambridge in England, a logician and probabilist. We are certain that Swamiji met Dr. John Venn in England, the renowned expert on logic and the author of "Logic of Chance," despite the fact that little is known about Swamji's interactions with any notable mathematicians or probabilists in the West. After this outstanding logician, the Venn diagrams—an integral component of probability theory—were called. Swamiji "impressed the professor very much, and he was most pleased with the encounter," according to Mahendranath Datta's (Swamiji's younger brother) testimony. Given their shared admiration, it wouldn't be far-fetched to argue that they were Probabilists from the East and the West who met.

Epilogue

We are simply perplexed as to the source of such power as we consider Swamiji's unusual capacity to mastery even a secular subject such as probability theory. On this extraordinary quality of Swamiji, Sister Christine offers an interpretative observation: "Others may be brilliant; his mind is luminous, for he had the capacity to bring himself into direct contact with the source of all knowledge. He is no longer constrained by the slow process to which regular people are subject.

So that's all, then! Living as he did in the radiant splendor of his own being, Swamiji's 'luminous' mind was constantly in contact with the source of knowledge, enabling him to master everything and everything with an effortless grace.

He truly is a superb example of how the Atmajnani (knower of the self) can simply acquire any knowledge if he so desires. It's hardly surprising that his advice in this regard (as usual) is backed up by his own firsthand knowledge: "Try to manifest this Atman, and you will see your intellect penetrating into all subjects." The genius of one who knows Atman is all-encompassing, in contrast to the one-sided intelligence of one who has not yet realized Atman. Science, philosophy, and everything else will be simple for you to master once the Atman manifests.

Let's use all of our resources to make this Atman manifest in all spheres of life, including academia. Then and only then can we consider ourselves to be deserving students of this master probabilist-sannyasi, for whom the only "certainty" amid the probabilistic uncertainties of phenomenal existence is "Atman," as he never tired of emphasizing: "The soul endureth forever."

CHAPTER FIVE
Swami Savior of Hinduism

They required a guide to show them the true purpose of living in a society where everyone was consumed by sensual pleasures and the materialistic race of living a luxury existence. While other religions just teach about spiritual understanding of peace, love, and the interrelationships of humanity; they only focus on the body and its pleasures, Hinduism addresses the body, mind, and soul. Swami Vivekanand popularized the ideas of unity, the soul, and the one and only purpose of human birth. People all across the world were enthralled by the novel idea and learned about the true regions of existence through Hinduism's spiritual science and meditation.

New Perspectives on the Dharma (Religion)

Swami Vivekananda's understanding of religion as a shared human experience of transcendent truth is one of his greatest contributions to the modern world. By demonstrating that Hinduism is as scientific as science itself—religion is the "science of consciousness," as Swamiji put it—he faced the challenge posed by modern science. As a result, religion and science are complementary rather than mutually exclusive.

Since religion is now seen as the highest and most noble pursuit—the pursuit of supreme freedom, supreme knowledge, and supreme happiness—it is liberated from the grip of superstitions, dogmatism, priestcraft, and bigotry.

New Perspective on Manhood

A new, elevated conception of man is presented by Vivekananda's Hindu concept of the "potential divinity of the soul." The current era is known as the age of humanism, which contends that man should be the primary focus of all endeavors and the center of all thought. Man has acquired immense riches and power through science and technology, and contemporary means of communication and travel have transformed human civilization into a "global village." But man's degeneration has also been progressing quickly, as evidenced by the huge rise in broken houses, immorality, violence, crime, etc. in contemporary society. This degeneration is avoided by Vivekananda's idea of the potential divinity of the soul, which also elevates interpersonal interactions and gives life purpose and value.

Swamiji provided the groundwork for "spiritual humanism," which is now taking shape in a number of neo-humanistic movements and the widespread interest in meditation, Zen, etc.

Hinduism's New Moral and Ethical Principles

The morality that predominates in both private and public life is mostly founded on fear: fear of the law, fear of public scorn, fear of God's wrath, dread of karma, etc. Additionally, it demonstrated that God himself summarized the idea to demonstrate his omnipotence and omnipresence rather than being founded on principles established by a single prophet or preacher. A person should be moral and kind to others, yet this is not explained by the contemporary conceptions of ethics followed by non-Hindus. Based on the inherent purity and unity of the Atman, Vivekananda developed a new philosophy of ethics and a new moral tenet.Because purity is our genuine nature, our authentic divine being, or Atman, we ought to be pure. As a result of our shared connection to the Supreme Spirit, also known as Paramatma or Brahma, we should also love and serve our neighbors.The Indian youth has simply forgotten his aspirations to transform Bharat into the perfect country. Hindu youngsters were encouraged to learn about our most important texts after Swamiji helped non-Hindus realize that many of their scientific theories were derived from Hindu scriptures.

CHAPTER SIX
The Smritis and The Puranas

The Smritis and the Puranas were composed for laypeople and passed down orally from one generation to the next. Higher scriptures like the Aranyakas (theologies) and Upanishads (philosophy) are complex and need in-depth study to comprehend their meaning. The Pauranic fables were created to aid understanding of more complicated concepts found in literature like the Vedas for simple people who are most likely unable to decipher the deeper meaning of these texts.

The Vishnu Purana and Bhagwad Purana, for example, are the scriptures of the Vaishnavism sect. The Puranas were primarily designed to inspire love and respect for the God they worship. Lord Vishnu has been prominently featured in them. The tales center on Lord Vishnu's majesty and excellence. Similar to this, Lord Shiva is depicted as the most powerful god in the Shiva Purana, Lingam Purana, etc. They serve as the Shaivism sect's founding texts. The Adi Shakti's sovereignty is also made clear in the Devi Purana, for example. Due to these stories in the Puranas and Smritis demonstrating a bias towards a certain god or goddess, conflicts frequently break out between various groups. The Vedas assert that the Nirguna Brahman is the only source of perfect truth, therefore how can a formless God have various manifestations?

The fundamental notion is that all deities are representations of the ultimate Parabrahman. They each excel in their respective capacities and perform various roles. Discrimination develops as a result of ignorance. The stories found in the Puranas are logically constrained. In the words of Swami Vivekananda, "Only parts of them breathing broadness of spirit and love are acceptable; the rest are to be rejected."Thus, the Vedas are the primary source for learning Hinduism. Therefore, under the direction of a knowledgeable spiritual master, the Vedas and Upanishads are always a good place to start if one wants to study Hinduism.

CHAPTER SEVEN
Vedas-Introduction

Without the assistance of a knowledgeable guru, it is difficult to read and nearly impossible to comprehend the Vedas. Vaidik Sanskrit, which differs greatly from conventional Sanskrit, is used to produce the Vaidik Sanhitas in particular. They are poetically subtle, nuanced, and intricate. Every line in the Vedas is said to contain seven levels of secret meaning. The Devas communicate in this way, using multiple interwoven levels while bringing forth parallels and affinities in the natural world to express highly developed thoughts. The majority of human minds are unable to comprehend such discourse.

Because of this, several translations of the Vedas have come off as odd or absurd in various contexts. It necessitates years of immersion in traditional training as well as the development of a distinctively Vedic way of thinking, both of which can only be acquired by residing in such a culture. It is frequently impossible for people who were raised in other cultures, such as western or westernized cultures, to ever acquire, despite their best efforts.

The mantras of the Vedas, especially the Sanhitas, are traditionally utilized for the spiritual potency of their sounds alone rather than typically trying to understand their meanings for all the reasons listed above and more.

The Bhagavad Gita, the Vedanta Sutras, the Agamas, Puranas, and Itihasas, as well as other smritis and shastras, were all created in much simpler language to clarify the basic meaning of the Vedas in Hinduism.

Hindus have mostly studied those for thousands of years. Few people have attempted to understand the meaning of the Vedic sounds, yet they have conserved them and used them in Yagnya. Only a limited group of experts who had been schooled from birth could achieve that, and at this point in the Kaliyuga, even their understandings may be in doubt.

CHAPTER EIGHT
Vedas

1. The Rig Veda The most important part of the Vedas is a collection of enlightening mantras or sktas, which are verses called riks (ric, rik, or rig—verse) dedicated to the devas or gods. In these hymns, the Riis, or sages, express their spiritual encounters while they are in heightened stages of concentration.

2. Sma-veda: texts of happy, choral chants called smans that are meant to be sung to specific melodies a version of the Rig Veda that has been divided up and organized so that it can be sung during the numerous Vedic sacrifices.

3. The writings of sacrifice rituals or "yajus," or the appropriate ordaining of conduct, are found in the Yajur Veda. It primarily consists of prayers and invocations that are appropriate for the consecration of the tools and materials used in sacrifice worship but also serve as reminders of

the path to becoming divine for man. 'The White' and 'The Black' are the two sections that make up this Veda.

4. The Atharva-Veda is a collection of holy scriptures that contain mystical formulas and chants to be recited for special occasions like weddings, births, and funerals. These texts also provide formulas for fending off chaos-causing energies and karmic illnesses.

These Vedas are split into four sections:

1. Mantras or sktas: lyrical songs of adoration

2. brhmaas: literary compositions that include stories, myths, explanations, theology, philosophy, and traditional material while also addressing Vedic rituals.

3. Rayakas, which are treatises on philosophical and religious topics related to the Brahmanas and intended for study by forest ascetics.

4. Upaniads: Poetry and prose works on intellectual, religious, and spiritual topics

Key Upanishads

Aitareya, Kauitaki, Taittiriya, Kaha, Maitri, Bhadarayaka, Vetvatara, Chogya, Kea, Tlavakra, Muaka, Mukya, and Prana are some of the other names for themselves.

Smaller Upanishad

Amta-bindu, Tejo-bindu, Skanda, rrik, Garbha, Nda-bindu, Nryaa, Sarva-sra, Ailya, Bhikuka, Hasa, Maala-brahma, Maitreya, Vajra-sci, Dhyna-bindu, Yoga-tattva, Amta-nda, Varha, Yoga-kuali, Muktika, Nirlamba, Paingala, Adhytma, Subala, Tra-sra, Bhikuka, and Tra-sra

UPA VEDAS

āyur-Veda — Scripture dealing with medicine.

Dhanur Veda — Scripture dealing with archery.

śastra-śāstra — *Scripture dealing with martial arts.*

gāndharva-Veda — *Scripture of music.*

sthāpatya-Veda — *Scripture of architecture.*

śilpa-śāstra — *Scripture of fine arts.*

The GRIHYA SUTRAS, which cover the guidelines for home rituals and ceremonies, are referred to by the names of their authors: -

Kauitaki, Avalayana, ankhyana, Baudhyana, pastamba, Hirayakein, Bhradvja, Satyasadha, Vaikhnasa, Parkara, Gobhila, Khadira, Jaimini, Kauika

DHARMA SHASTRAS—Books on law

similar to the aforementioned authors, with Manu added.

BIG PURANAS

Agni Brahm, Brahma-vaivarta, Vmana, Brahma, Mrkaeya, Bhaviya, Viu, Bhgavata, Padma, Nradiya, Garua, Varha Matsya, Liga, Skanda, Krma, and Iva

TANTRAS

Tantrarja Tantra, Viu Ymala Tantra, Kulasra Tantra, Rudra Ymala Tantra, Mahanirva Tantra, Prapacasra Tantra, Brahma Ymala Tantra, Kulrava Tantra, Todala Tantra

AGAMAS

Śaiva āgama:- sūkṣma, kāmika, yogarāja, cintya, kāraṇa, ajita, dīpta, sahasra, aṁśumat and suprabheda.
Rudra āgama:— vijaya, nihśvāsa, svayambhūva, anala, vīra,

raurava, makuṭha, vimala, candrajñāna, mukhabhimbha, prodgīta, lalita, sidda, santāna, śarvokta, pārameśvara, kiraṇa and vātula

Pañcarātra āgama:— *īśvara saṁhita, parama saṁhita, bṛihad brahma saṁhita, pauṣkara saṁhita, sāttvata saṁhita, jñānāmṛtasāra saṁhita, agastya saṁhita, aniruddha saṁhita, ahirbhudnya saṁhita, kapiñjala saṁhita, kāśyapa saṁhita, jayākhya saṁhita, jñānāmṛtasāra saṁhita, nāradīya saṁhita, paramapuruṣa saṁhita, parāśara saṁhita, pādma saṁhita, pārameśvara saṁhita, puruṣottama pauṣkara bhāradvāja, mārkaṇḍeya, lakṣmī tantra, viśvamitra viṣṇu-tilaka, viṣṇu, viṣvaksena, śāṇḍilya, śeṣa, śrīpraśna saṁhita, sanatkumāra & hayaśīrṣa samhita*

Ramayana and Mahabharata (which includes the Bhagavad Gita)

3. Yoga-Vasiha: A 32,000-line poem by Vlmiki that explores profound practical mysticism, grand intellectual ideas, and literary beauty. The 'crown jewel' of Vedanta works, as some have dubbed it. It is Rama's inner spiritual tale.

4. Harivaa, a reimagining of Ka and his hobbies' stories

COMMUNITY SCIENCES

1. The Kama-sutra, a work on eugenics and erotica by the wise Vtsyyana

2. Artha-stra: A treatise on the science of politics by Kauhilya that discusses both economic life and politics.

3. Brihatsahita, a book by Varhamihira that covers a variety of scientific subjects like astrology, astronomy, and other knowledge.

4. Nti stra, also known as the "Ethical Scripture," is a body of literature that discusses moral and prudent conduct, political insight, moral philosophy, and precepts (n—to lead, direct).

The sayings of Cnakya Pait are the most well-known of them.

5. The Garland of Birth-Stories, or Jtaka Ml, contains the accounts of Buddha's several earthly incarnations.

6. Books of moralized tales created to teach young princes appropriate behavior.

7. The "Book of Good Counsel," also known as "Htopadea" (hita-upadea), is a compilation of animal tales that offer princes wise counsel. Many of Aesop's fables were inspired by this book. Other collections include Kath-sarit-sgara, Ocean of Rivers of Stories by Somadeva, Bhat-kath-majar by Kemendra, and Vehla-pacaviati, "A Demon's 25 Stories."

CHAPTER NINE
Sprituality Philosophy

Swami Vivekananda's contribution to modern spiritual philosophy is his understanding of Vedanta. He decided to call his activity in America's organizational framework the Vedanta Society. Although we are aware of what a "society" is, we must consider the type of "Vedanta" that Swamiji had in mind when he used the term in relation to his Western works.

our will enable us to comprehend the function of Vedanta societies in our nation. Additionally, it will answer the issues and inquiries that many Vedanta students have regarding the meaning of the term "Vedanta student." Does that imply that I am a Hindu by default? Can I practice Vedanta without identifying as Hindu? These issues require investigation. Our understanding of Vedanta can be found in Vivekananda's interpretation of it.

We must acknowledge right away that the word "Vedanta" carries a variety of meanings. For many people, the word has varied connotations. It is feasible to state that there are three main uses for the word Vedanta.

Hinduism and Vedanta as One Religion

The Upanishads, a group of texts that are a component of the Vedas, the primary scripture of the Hindus, are where Vedanta is best expressed as the philosophy that governs life on the Indian subcontinent. Another term for the Upanishads is Vedanta (Veda + anta), as they often occur at the end (anta) of the Vedas and are said to embody the essence (anta) of the Vedas.

But neither the Vedas nor the Upanishads are actually "books." No books are intended by the Vedas, according to Vivekananda. They refer to the collection of spiritual laws that have been learned over time by various individuals. The Vedic knowledge was verbally passed down from generation to generation before it was recorded in writing. According to its etymology, the word Upanishad refers to knowledge that liberates people from existential pain annihilates the seeds of material existence, and points people in the direction of the Supreme Being. As a result, the Upanishads or Vedanta are only books in a tangential sense.

The fact that the term "Hindu" does not appear once in the traditional Hindu scriptures is now widely acknowledged. Hindus today's ancestors did not consider themselves to be Hindus. Persians are the source of the word "Hindu".

The people who resided on the other side of the river Sindhu were referred to as "Hindu" by them. The people who lived along the banks of the river Sindhu came to be known as Hindus because they pronounced the letter "s" with a "h" sound. The "h" vanished, the river became the Indus, and the inhabitants were referred to as "Indians" when the British occupied the area. Hinduism is the term used by Western academics and Christian missionaries to refer to the predominant religion of India. According to Swami Vivekananda, the name of the religion should be Vaidika Dharma and the title of the population should be Vaidikas or, more precisely, Vedantists.

First and foremost among the characteristics shared by the various traditions that have developed within Hinduism is their devotion to the Vedas. A tradition is no longer regarded as "Hindu" if it rejects the validity of the Vedas. Due to this, Hinduism and Vedanta are considered to be the same thing in Indian culture. Although it must be acknowledged that the majority of Indians who were brought up in the religion of the Vedas would identify themselves as Hindus rather than Vedantists, these two titles refer to the same religious tradition. It is clear why this is the case. The terms "Hindu" and "Hinduism" have been used more frequently in modern speech and literature than "Vedanta." They now form a part of the language that is widely used.

Vedanta as a Part of Hinduism

It is simple to classify Vedanta as just one of the many schools or sects within Hinduism if we ignore the word's historical roots and the true meaning of the term "Vedanta." Therefore, mentioning the Vedanta tradition in the same sentence as the Shaiva tradition, the Shakta tradition, the Tantrik tradition, or the Vaishnava tradition is not unusual. If the classification is based on the object of devotion, then individuals who worship Vishnu, Narayana, or, more commonly,

Rama or Krishna, are considered Vaishnavas. Shaivas are people who worship Shiva as their main deity. Shaivas are people who worship Shiva as their main deity. The goddess, who may take the form of Kali or Durga, has a central place in the Shakta and Tantrik traditions. The impersonal Supreme Being, also known as Paramatman or Brahman, is regarded as the ideal in the Vedanta school, which follows a similar line of reasoning.

About the Author

Saurabh Suman

Saurabh Suman has worked in various MNCs as engineers and in managerial positions in the past 10 years including roles of a business analyst, business development manager, brand analyst, & market researcher for various firms.

He has been a content writer for multiple companies as well. He excels in content writing & content marketing.He was awarded the Rising Young Author Award 2022 at the Constitution Club of India by the Honorable Speaker of the Delhi Assembly, Shri Ramniwas Goyel, from the National Achiever's Recognition Forum in 2022 for publishing 28 novels in the shortest period. And also received Top 100 Author of India in 2023.

And he was also invited by the Electoral Club of Parul University as an honorable guest at Parul University, Vadodara, Gujarat, as a speaker for an iconic talk on

Loktantra and as a guest speaker on World Environment Day 2024. He was also invited to be a sports enthusiast at ITM (SLS) University on World Health Day 2024. Saurabh was born into a middle-class family in Bihar. He completed his schooling at different schools: Bishop Westcott, Ranchi, Jharkhand, Assembly of God Church School , Bettiah , Bihar, and Patna Central School, Patna, Bihar. During his management studies, he penned down his first novel, "When Life Starts Playing," of which the book review was published by The Times of India, The Speaking Tree (PAGE 3).

www.ingramcontent.com/pod-product-compliance
Lightning Source LLC
LaVergne TN
LVHW041639070526
838199LV00052B/3464